THE 11TH HOUR MEETUP

THE 11TH HOUR MEETUP A FICTIONAL TO REAL WORLD CONNECTION BASED STORY

VIVEK VALSARAJ

THIS BOOK IS DEDICATED TO ALL MY LOVING ONES AND ALSO TO HATERS

SEE , HERE I HAVE DONE IT?

V

Contents

Preface

This is the first book i have written , with totally different taste , probably ,

or i can say surely it is one the list of nonexistence book ever before , i have put

my all best words , thoughts while writing this book , this will be one of the wonderful book

including full of taste of love , war, how to handle situation , loyalty and many more things .

LUCY - MY DOG

JACK - AUTHOR NAME

ROSE - AUTHOR'S CLASSMATE

Acknowledgements

One people can't do all things but but if someone support then they can do.

I would like to say thanks to my brother , father , friends who supported me for

writing this wonderful story .... thanks again everyone

special thanks to all my dear readers

Introduction

THIS IS SHORT FICTIONAL STORY BUT NOT LESS THAN REAL ,

YOU WILL SEE , HOW THINGS CHANGED , IMPORTANCE OF OUR CLOSE ONE,

LUCY - NAME OF AUTHOR'S DOG

JACK - NAME OF AUTHOR

ROSE - AUTHOR CLASSMATE

ONE

SCARY OR SATISFYING NIGHT

I am the author of this story ? It wonder, i am telling this to you , a fictional story

but not less than a real one .

It was raining all where, dark everywhere , wind was blustery , i was looking from

window , it was like window will go off , a agressive air crossing the window and my jacket ,

all were flapping heavly weather was too cold , my mom had set bonefire , that was giving

some heat, it was the situation somewhere between scary or satisfying ? I am not wholly sure

about this , but i am sure it was challenging .

i was a common , not a special man , my father was an army officer , he had'nt returned to home

, past 10 years due to so busy duty .

me , my mom , my lucy (dog) , and two darkest room , it was all together with us only.

I looked sometimes through window on another time , i look at my lucy (dog) ,

in between , my mind reminds is it streak of luck , viz. We are far from street noise, an apocalyptic

environment or a tragedy ; that we are apart from social interaction of society , and living at this

silent place .

beside all of these , i register by god grace, we are breathing so pure air here , at that time rain intensity

reduced, my lamp light was about to turned off , night was merely scary or satisfying , it was probably between it. my luy (dog) started barking like , he would call for dinner , at the same time

my mom scolded ;

- Mom - c'mon , jack dinner is all set .

- Me - yes Mom , i am right there soon .

- Mom- Lucy you too come for dinner .

- Me- sprinkled water on eyes , sat on dinning chair , gazing at roof silently ,

feeling like roof was saying something not thunderous but in soothing way .

- Mom- Jack arrange the plate , took out breaad and put in plate .

- Me- yes mom feeling butterfly fying in my stomach , i started eating .

- Mom - Jack don't eat like a horse or you may go under weather .

- Me - oh , yeah mom , okay all aright.

afterward i went in my room , sat on chair , open my notebook , started writing

my daily diary as usual , i used to write .

My mind swirl , i wonder , like my inner voice saying , does my existence really matters,

this type of thought hadn't ever come in mind previously
.

well , let it be ! I will deal or miracle will happen , i m going to win from all , at the end .

TWO

NEXT MORNING

Window was open , ray was falling on my eyes sharply , making

uncomfortable for sleeping for more further few minutes , simultaneously ,

Mom scolded ,

- Mom - Wake up Jack , it is going late for your college,

  you are so behind time Jack.

- Me - oh mom C'mon , i woke up already , no need to tear your vocal cord.

After this , i went to washroom , opened tap , water was drizzling , i sprinkled water

on my face , I did cross all morning routine and sat on chair , my lucy (dog)

came there , i gently blowed my hand on his hair , me and my lucy palyed some minutes there,

i was so connected to my Lucy , he was a like a close member of family.

after this mom brought breakfast , i took and went and stepped forward for college.

College was 500 metre apart from my home , when i reached there, there was a lot of sound coming in ear,

as i was outside from my classroom too , it was like fish market.

As usual i met with my all friends including Rose (A fascinating girl of my class) ,

as she inetrrupted with ,

- Rose - hi Jack , how's going everything ?

- Me- yes Rose , fine , you say what about you, is everything okay ?

- She - yes Jack . all is fine as usual !

- Me- no Rose you are not on cloud nine as you usual , tell what happened?

- She - Jack if you want something, just say ; don't beat around the bush .

- Me- nothing special , i thought , something made you dizzy for a while , your mind

are engaged somewhere , you are not focused here ? it is really okay ? if not then you can share with me .

- She - nothing like that to reveal , i am here , change the topic , let me go out for while , i will be soon connecting to you , bye for now !

- After this she went for washroom , i noticed her eyes were watery , i dont know the exact reason and i didn't prefer to ask about the eaxct reason.

But i could see the substitute of some matter on her eyes.
she came after a while behaved like a normal , so i also ignored and didn't ask again.
after some time she break the ice and replied , all okay , and if not then what will you do ?

- I replied back don't say like this , i am ready to stand by you in every situation , despite of

  situation.

- she replied " yes i will share at right time "
- I too replied " as you like " as your wish !

after class , we went for a tea , but in my mind her unrevealed thoughts were drifting ,

- i was so eager to know the exact reason of her saddness ,

in between all she said me , "lets go on mountain " for refreshment at today evening .

- I replied back " yes" why not ?

THREE

A BEAUTIFUL SCENERY

We went on evening for mountain scenery ,

walking together, on unwalked road ;

her hand was in my hand, the magical evening sparkling

like bright star ;

It seemed , road was endless with love paved on so beautifully;

her hand was locked in my hand, like it will never ever seperate;

she was saying something , but my mind was not listening , only eyes were starring

on her face , how cutely she was speaking,;

her voice was so sexy , and probably her words would be truely about something on healthy subject ;

but who cares ! all are quite flavourless in sight of her face ;

she was really so thinker and deep listener , because she always take a big gap between speaking

something;

If i would say about her beauty , my mind never refuse to the fact that, mirror would never seen

this type of drop dead gorgeous lady ever before;

Her beauty was not less than angelic or i can say more than that;

my heart wanted to pronounced, I love you dear , but my minds stopped for doing this act

at this time ;

i can't measure her whole goodness , her whole streched beauty;

In life sometimes we win , we lose , but in this case , i can never think of losing her,

i have never seen such a cute, precious peace , splendid girl;

A well crafted girl , so much characteristic as she was full of ,

really an unxceptional in whole universe.

I was decided , once i will hold her hand , and will never leave in future,

i will too never turn back from all the promises i will make ;

I will apologies , even she will make mistakes in future , but never

thinking of retracing from all of these promises which i will make;

I would hope she would never injured the feelings of mine in future;

I know if we made mistakes , it can't be reversed , but i hope never make that mistakes again,

i will never forget , she pushed me off so many times to come out from dark ,

i became irresponsible for many times, but i was known she was behind for correction, i will never admit , she will leave me somedays ,

this time , sun had set , her face was becoming invisible due to dusk,

we had reached at mountain by this time, her hand was still cross linked in my hand ;

we sat there , talked about past , present , and more things ,

I said " you bring a smile on my face even in my worst situation ,

you always give crystal clear texture , everything belongs to mine ,

i will pray to God , never make other world for us , as we are one !

Really there's no end of joy when you spend beautiful time me.

We were starring in sky „ stars were twinkling , so satisfying

time that was !

my all stess , strain , vanished by seeing these two beautiful things

one is mountain , other is you !

it's not tough to go down from top of this mountain , but climbing was up

not easy , like that , it's easy to break any relation but it hards to join them;

that evening is so beautiful , i am so many splendid things at one time ,

twinkling stars , dazzling girl , a big mountain which are saying always go for up;

this all gives peace from all sorrow !

" lets go for home Jack " we are getting late , she said ,

and we turned back !

FOUR

NATURAL DISASTER

We returned from there and , i stepped back in my house , wall clock

was oscillating , tik tak tok sound were clearly hearable,

showing time 9PM , my poor old clock was till working , it had shown us many miserable moments,

never missed to remind walking , eating , sleeping on time , they always reminds my time ,

my moments , my condition , they teach me a lot , never in life be slow or fast , be always normal in

every situation , this is time man , changes always , they teaches no one is king , it's just a function of time

as time changed , situation and condition changed, so always be cool , never be too much happy ,

never be too much hopeless man. let's see me , i am old still never disappointed from my life , i am

still showing right time , like me , you should be cool in every situation dear !

I went in my room , sitting on chair , and recalling my mind what to write down on my diary after dinner, in between all , sounds from sky came like firecracker burst in sky ,

light started flashing , window start beating since very truculent wind stroke on !

combination of thunder , light and rain came , situation was between wonderous and scary ,

i saw a violence of storms , sky was starry , my mom closes the door , but that violent air

was so hasty , that smashed my firmly fixed door, entry of wind could be compared with demons

who came , and want to kill , tear down all !

Ah! this spine chilling , blood curdling , environment made me so strained !

on the land of silence , wizardous rain approached and " Break the ice "

like the heart burst , water, water pourdown everywhere .

with quiteness , My mind recalls " Hey God Mercy on us , if you would so good,

give some reassurance from this measury , give some strength , so we will

get away from this tragic !

My mom was preparing for get away from here,

she took Lucy (my dog) , and started running from home , she was so terrified ,

like someone take out roots from plant, her eyes was filled with salty water , and flowing like flood ,

she probably tasted it !

she was vey likely , noiselessly questioning to supreme being , why ? why? all tragic drama happen

with my nuclear family . On the other contrary , devine being was like reactionless . Yet we take receipt of confront and eventually we shared out these complication and came

out from our home , i will not go at length , how we leaked out from home , aside from

all reached out at pacifying site , by " God grace" .

But our Lucy Met with accident in these trrouble , we took him to hospital ,

he got hospitalised , THIS WAS LIKE ONE OF THE 11TH OUR MEETUP ,

HOW IS IT ? WILL BE SHARED IN NEXT CHAPTER .

FIVE

THE 11TH HOUR MEETUP

We took our Lucy in hospital , he was in care of doctor now ,

but after sometime doctor came called , we haven't saved our dog , if you were

at hospital 30 minutes earlier then we would probably save ! but sorry we can't !

me and my mom started crying , so much ! but what could be done now , things had

gone from our hand ;

I was remembering the moment we spent with our dog ,

he was so kind and faithful toward us , just a family member,

whenever i reached at home , he came , played a lot , whenever i was sleeping at late ,

he chewed my blanket , they start barking till my waking up ,

i know if he would be no more , we will missed a much ,

i can't express , many times he understood my mood , he was like my best friend forever , his loyalty with our family was so indeeed,

whenever , weather was cold , he behave like he is saying take me on your bed !

i feed clean always to him , when he was thirst ;

we walked with him so long a mile at morning ;

he made my routine so well maintained ;

i never saw him like a animal ;

he was so layal and well trained , so obeyed , so intelligent dog;

this was one of the great loss of my family from this ,

really his loyalty towards our family was incredible ;

he was probably missing us from heaven ;

why God , why you took our so beloved things so soon ;

if we reached to hospital 30min before , doctor would surely save him ; but we

reached at 11th hour , there will always a regret for this whole life ;

we lost a gem from our home !

We lost another important person's mom that is Rose's mom

how these things happened between this will be shared in next part of this book !

Will Be Continued

we will share another 11th hour meetup and how we lost Rose's mom

in next part this was the first part of this book .

ONE THING I HAD TO ASK?

DO YOU REALLY WANT NEXT PART THEN
NEVER FORGET TO GIVE FEEDBACK

Printed by Libri Plureos GmbH in Hamburg,
Germany